Chipper Ch

Book 1: The Birthday Surprise

By Stuart Parry

illustrations - Shanaka Thiara

contact - stuart@chipperchimp.com

ISBN - 9798718794922

Dedication..!

I want to dedicate this book to my two peeps!

About the Author

Stuart has always loved to make little poems and rhymes. In the past, many of his works manifested in the form of birthday cards, Christmas cards, Valentine's Day cards, etc. It wasn't until he began reading books to his young son Thomas, did he realise the enjoyment that comes from reading poems and bedtime books. He decided to turn his hand to writing fun rhyming picture books that parents can read to their children and send their little ones to bed with a smile on their faces.

Chipper the cheeky Chimpanzee
Is a mischievous little soul,
With his cheeky face and playful ways
The days are never droll.

On this bright and sunny morning,
He could hardly contain his glee,
For he knew, just one sleep away
He would turn from two to three.

Tomorrow is his birthday
And he thought that he might pop,

As the excitement rose and rose and rose
But was already at the top.

So he tried to think of things to do
To pass away the day,
And thought, "I know I'll find my friends
And ask them out to play."

OFF he swung from tree to tree
To see who he could see,

At last, he found the lion pride
But where could Eddie be?

"Oooo ahh ahh," he said
As he addressed the snoozing King,
"Your majesty, can you help me?
Eddie has gone missing."

"Edward is his name"
The King corrected with a growl,
"I haven't seen him all day long"

"...but what's that behind your tail?"

So off our Chipper swung
To find another pal,
"I know who always wants to play
My friend Archie the owl."

Arriving at the tree
Where Archie's parents like to stay,
He politely said to Mrs owl
"Is Archie Free to play?"

"To whit to whoo
Good day to you
I'm afraid he's just not in,"
"Okay, I'll find another friend

...but what's that behind your wing?"

Undeterred by the gracious bird
Through the trees, he swung once more
Until he saw
On the Forest Floor the tail of Mr Boar.

The large round hog was deep in a bog
Of mud the only sound a snuffle,
His huge appetite was craving a bite
Of his favourite food the truffle.

“Mr Boar good day I hope you are okay,
Is my friend Esmay free to play?”

“Snuffle snort I’m afraid you are a little too late,
she is out with her mummy all day.”

"Oh well" sighed Chipper
"I'm sorry to disturb
Your hunt for that food so smelly"
"I'll find another chum to have some fun
...But what's that behind your belly?"

With a hop, skip and jump
And the occasional bump,
Through the treetops he speedily traversed,

As he knew that for a laugh
His tallest friend Jerry giraffe,
Was head and shoulders above in first.

As the trees' edge drew near,
Where the leaves had disappeared,
He knew he'd found the place they liked to eat,
As he looked around and found
Standing six metres off the ground
Jerry's dad with a mouth full of his favourite treat.

Chipper said, "Afternoon,
do those trees need such a prune,
And is my friend Jerry free to have a laugh?"
(Chomp chomp) "It's getting late,"
said Mr giraffe as he ate,
"Jerry can't play as he is in his bubble bath."

"Okay, well never mind,
Today my friends are hard to find,
I'm starting to worry if there might be something wrong.
Ahh! I guess it's alright,
I think I'll head home for the night,
...but what's that hiding behind that neck of yours so long?"

So he did just as he said,
And headed home to his warm bed,
For he knew his birthday was almost here at last.

He got all safe and snug,
After a favourite mummy hug,
And some nice warm milk served in his favourite glass.

He tried his best to sleep,
He counted lots of jumping sheep,
But he couldn't find a slumber very deep.

He found it hard to keep,
His eyes closed without a peep,
As excitement made his heart flutter and leap.

At last, the morning came,
The excitement was hard to contain,
He was out of bed and down the stairs in flight.

The curtains were shut tight,
The room was dark as the darkest night,
And his parents were strangely nowhere near in sight.

It was then with such a fright,
The room lit up with a bright light,
The bangs and whistles filled the room in such a way.

All his friends were cheering loud,
A fantastic, joyful, happy crowd,
Then all as one they sang... HAPPY BIRTHDAY!

Notes...

Please when you are able, take a few minutes to read about a Little girl named Isla Caton who is very dear to many people

Isla is a 6 year old girl who has been fighting Neuroblastoma since the age of 2. Neuroblastoma is a rare form of childhood cancer and sadly has no cure to date.

Trials are available OUTSIDE the U.K.

Isla has been to Barcelona and was there for 2 years having these trials and at times became cancer free and in remission. Sadly that's no longer the case and we are fundraising again now to help her and her fight against this horrible disease.

20% of all proceeds from this book will be donated to Isla Caton

You can read more about Isla, follow her progress and if able, donate with the below details

Twitter @islasfight

Insta @teamislacaton

Thank you

Stuart

Printed in Great Britain
by Amazon